To all the children who read this book, this is dedicated to you. Each one of you is magical! Always believe and always let your sparkle shine.

ISBN number 978-1-912180-04-2

E book ISBN number 978-1-912180-05-9

Printed in the UK

Design by Steve Swinden, 2016 (sswinden53@gmail.com)

Illustrated by Cintia Sand.

Archangel Raguel Brings Harmony

Carrie M Bush

Feathers will find you always

when I'm near

Sometimes a rainbow will appear

A star may twinkle

Some glitter may sprinkle

Music may play

All to show you I'm with you

each day

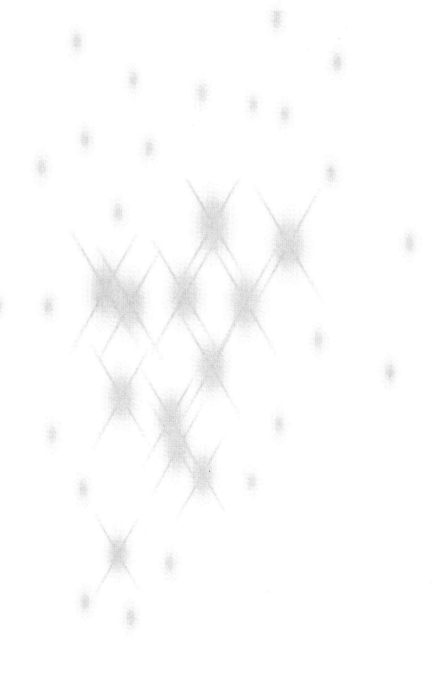

Archangel Raguel Brings Harmony

Gabby was excited. Tonight was the opening night of the school production, *Alice the Musical*. She had been busy all week practicing her lines. She had the main part of Alice. Gabby had always loved singing and acting, and was especially looking forward to performing for an audience.

Archangel Raguel Brings Harmony

Archangel Raguel Brings Harmony

Today had been a busy afternoon of rehearsals, while the other students were finishing things and setting the stage. Earlier in the day Gabby had been practicing. She was to close the show with a song, and this was the bit Gabby was most excited about; the spotlight would be on her, and she would be the star.

Archangel Raguel Brings Harmony

Archangel Raguel Brings Harmony

She could picture her parents' faces being proud of her. Miss Webb, the music teacher, came to speak with Gabby. "We have been talking, and we think it could be a good idea if Ella sang Alice's final song with you? We thought it may sound nicer as a duet," she said. Gabby felt cross. She didn't want Ella to share the spotlight; she wanted to be the star of the show. Miss Webb could see the frustration in her face, so she said, "It is your choice, Gabby; have a little think about it."

Archangel Raguel Brings Harmony

Archangel Raguel Brings Harmony

Gabby didn't need time to think; she loved Ella as a friend, but there was no way she was sharing this with her! As Miss Webb turned to leave she said, "Gabby, you could always ask the archangels for some help to make the right decision." Miss Webb was such a lovely, kind teacher, and often after lessons she would sit with her students and talk about the angels. She would tell everyone the ways in which they could help. The students loved listening to Miss Webb and hearing about the things that the angels had helped her with.

Archangel Raguel Brings Harmony

Archangel Raguel Brings Harmony

Gabby decided she didn't need the angels' help today; she told Miss Webb she wanted to sing the song alone. Miss Webb said that was absolutely fine, and she would go and tell Ella. A little later that afternoon, Gabby saw Ella was upset; she was disappointed at not getting the chance to sing in the show. Gabby tried to gently explain to her how excited she was to be closing the show on her own and how hard she had been rehearsing. Ella did not want to listen; she told Gabby she was being horrible, and both girls ended up arguing.

Archangel Raguel Brings Harmony

A few times in the afternoon Gabby tried to talk with Ella, but she just turned her head away from her each time. Gabby started to feel sad. She didn't want to lose Ella as a friend, but she really wanted to sing alone, and she didn't know what she should do.

Archangel Raguel Brings Harmony

Archangel Raguel Brings Harmony

Gabby decided she would go to speak with Miss Webb. "Are you ok, Gabby?" she said, seeing the worried look on her face.

"Ella won't talk to me," Gabby said, with tears welling up in her eyes. Miss Webb sat and listened quietly while she explained all about the argument.

After some time, Miss Webb gave her a gentle pat on her arm, "Gabby, it's never nice having an argument with a friend, so I know how upset you must be feeling. Why don't you call on Archangel Raguel? He will help you."

Archangel Raguel Brings Harmony

Archangel Raguel Brings Harmony

"How?" Gabby asked.

"He is the archangel of fairness, justice and harmony, and he can help you to resolve an argument," Miss Webb said.

She went on to tell Gabby his colour was a beautiful sky blue when he was around you, and he might be the right angel to help. Gabby thanked Miss Webb. She decided she would ask Archangel Raguel, she sat down on the floor in a corner of the hall and silently prayed in her head; she asked him to show her how to make Ella become her friend again.

Archangel Raguel Brings Harmony

Archangel Raguel Brings Harmony

Later, near the end of the school day, the
children started to pack up their bags. Miss
Webb asked them all to be back in school
that evening at 6pm to make time for having
make up and changing into their costumes
so there would be time before the production
started at 7pm. All the children rushed home
excitedly.

 Archangel Raguel Brings Harmony

Archangel Raguel Brings Harmony

Gabby walked past Ella. "See you tonight, Ella," she said.

Ella didn't say a word; she just walked away with a sad look in her eyes.

Miss Webb walked past Gabby to go to her car. "See you later, and don't worry. Everything will be just fine!" she said with a wink.

Archangel Raguel Brings Harmony

Archangel Raguel Brings Harmony

That evening after make up, Gabby and the cast were getting ready for the show to begin. Gabby started to feel a little nervous and decided she would step outside to the playground for some fresh air. As she sat on a bench, she looked up to the clouds and silently asked the angels to help her perform well in the show.

Archangel Raguel Brings Harmony

Archangel Raguel Brings Harmony

The clouds were big and fluffy and almost covered the whole sky. The sun was still warm for the summer evening. Gabby closed her eyes, and took a deep breath of fresh air, and, as she opened her eyes suddenly the clouds parted and, sparkling through, was a pale blue sky.

Archangel Raguel Brings Harmony

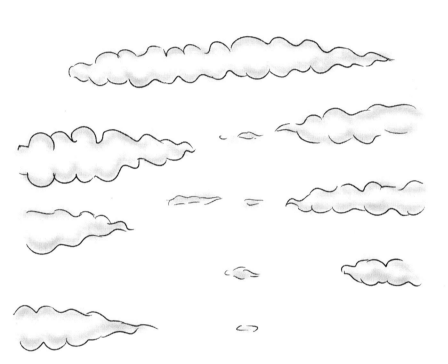

Archangel Raguel Brings Harmony

Gabby noticed the cloud was in the shape of a heart. She stared in wonder; she had never seen the sky look like this before, and had never seen a heart-shaped cloud.

Archangel Raguel Brings Harmony

Archangel Raguel Brings Harmony

She ran inside and found Miss Webb next to the stage busily ushering the children to their correct places. The hall was beginning to fill up with parents.

Gabby saw her mum and dad and gran waving over excitedly; they had managed to get seats in the front row!

Archangel Raguel Brings Harmony

Archangel Raguel Brings Harmony

Gabby quickly told Miss Webb about the heart shape in the cloud and the pale blue sky that seemed to sparkle. Miss Webb stood with a beaming smile. "Oh, that's definitely a sign from Archangel Raguel! Well done, Gabby," she said.

"Now let's get on with the show..."

Archangel Raguel Brings Harmony

Archangel Raguel Brings Harmony

The time seemed to go very fast, and all the parents were enjoying the show.

The children had remembered their lines, and Miss Webb sat proudly smiling in the front row. Gabby was standing at the side of the stage getting ready for her final song, when suddenly she felt someone brush her arm.

As she turned around to see who it was, she could not see anyone. She felt a warm feeling of love around her. Gabby smiled to herself; she just knew it was Archangel Raguel next to her.

Archangel Raguel Brings Harmony

She knew what she must do. She took

centre stage, and when she looked out to the

audience - she was shocked to see so many

people. She took the microphone and started

to speak.

"I would like to sing this final song with my

best friend Ella. I hope that you will all love

it!" Ella looked over; completely shocked,

she made her way up to the stage and stood

next to Gabby.

Archangel Raguel Brings Harmony

Archangel Raguel Brings Harmony

The music started and the girls began to sing. The song was beautiful, and both girls got a standing ovation at the end. Everyone was cheering and whistling and Gabby could even see her gran jumping up and down!

Archangel Raguel Brings Harmony

Archangel Raguel Brings Harmony

Ella turned to Gabby. "Thank you so much, you are such a good friend!" she said.

Gabby smiled. "There is no one I would want to share this with but you." Ella threw her arms around Gabby's neck, almost squashing her, she was hugging so tight!

Archangel Raguel Brings Harmony

Archangel Raguel Brings Harmony

Gabby looked over to Miss Webb, who was still clapping wildly. She looked straight into Gabby's eyes and gave her a big wink.

Archangel Raguel Brings Harmony

Archangel Raguel Brings Harmony

Gabby threw her head back, enjoying the moment, and she looked at the ceiling covered in blue flashing theatre lights that were sparkling everywhere!

She silently screamed thank you, thank you Archangel Raguel in her head. It was the best night of her life.

Archangel Raguel Brings Harmony

My angel wishes

My angel wishes

6 _____

7 _____

8 _____

9 _____

10 _____

If you enjoyed this book - you may also like:

Archangel Gabriel and the Dancer's Dream

Archangel Ariel Heals a Bird

Mia's Healing with Archangel Raphael

Archangel Metatron - The Fiery Angel

Archangel Raziel's Rainbow Bubble

Archangel Chamuel and the Lost Wish Box

Archangel Jophiel's Gift of Beauty and Joy

Archangel Haniel Brings Happiness

Archangel Azrael - Molly's Angel

Archangel Michael Saves the Day

Archangel Uriel Heals Eczema

Archangel Sandalphon's Magical Help

Willow Forgives with Archangel Zadkiel

Archangel Jeremiel Helps with Anxiety

For more information follow me on:

Twitter - @carriembush77
Facebook - https://m.facebook.com/CarrieMBush
Instagram - carriemariebush

May all your wishes come true...